PASSION AND RAGE

Portrait of an
Heroic Age Love
Trapped in the
Twentieth Century

MAGGIE VINCENTE

Maggie Vincente

Thank you to Debora, Inge, Janis, and Pamelann for your tireless editing help, in spite of my constant tweaking and reluctance to let go and call it "done". Special thanks go also to my amazing family for your constant love and support. You make this life most blessed,
and I love you all.

~~~~~~~~~

Original Manuscript Copyright 1998
Cover Illustration by M. Vincente, Copyright 1998
All Other Illustrations by M. Vincente, Copyright 2013

ISBN-13: 978-0615977737 (Old Knights Press)
ISBN-10: 0615977731

Library of Congress Catalog #TXu000777753 / 1997-01-10

Prologue

This is a story of heroic or "epic love" ~ that form which does not exist except as a function of its inherent intensity. Juliet and Romeo, Isolde and Tristan from the days of old ~ both couples personified epic love. The physical pain and anguish of separation was relieved only by an absolute and intertwining unity of bodies, minds, and souls. Failing the ability to hold such an ecstatic state, such a love was destined for doom.

In this modern age of an emphasis on personal control at all costs, such examples of cautionless passion and blinding rage may appear archaic. This story proves otherwise...

Maggie Vincente

Passion and Rage

Introduction
This diary contains precious memories…
handle with tender, loving care.

Written perceptions of moments lived
(and dreamed of) can be found in
earthtime chronological order.

Illustrations are sometimes included for reference
~ and to remind that this is Real.

Discretion must be maintained, of course,
but the Author remembers her Subject,
and her Subject remembers the Author.

"Nothing lasts Forever"… or does it?
Perhaps true believers will meet somewhere
again on another plane
in the time-space continuum.

"Until we meet again",
PEACE be with you, my Love.

Time Begins Now

Maggie Vincente

18 September…

Flying on a long, midnight journey
* to the farthest unknown*
*   reaches of bluest-black skies*
*   cool Spumante in sparkling flutes*
glistens in the starlight
* flowing through unshaded windows*
muted laughter from softened
* conversation of wit and wonder*
*   delights the ear and heart equally well*

Buoyed by rivulets of warm air,
* our craft gently*
*   sways into a rhythmic*
*   lullaby of whispered song*
moonlit clouds float by in unseen
* streams, casting fanciful*
*   illuminations on carpeted walls*
silken glances drift past
* half-lowered lashes, an embracing of*
*   other shadowed eyes*

…never enough…

Passion and Rage

<u>12 October</u>
Our eyes met across a
crowded plane
and locked in recognition.

Kindred souls,
once torn apart,
now reunited,
for a brief time only.

I knew your thoughts
as you knew mine
instantly and effortlessly.

The connection was whole and complete
in that moment
with no words
with no movement
with no missings.

14 November

*My knight in shining armour drives
  a battered Ford pickup.*

*He rescued this distressed damsel in front of
  the old south church at sunrise.*

*He soothed my tattered nerves with his quiet
  caresses as we zipped down the highway doing 50.*

*My hero delivered me safely into the regional airport.
He walked hand-in-hand with me to the
  car rental counter.
When these further vehicles failed to provide a
suitable means of immediate escape from my
tormentor, my hero bravely returned me to my
  tower of captivity, and my absent gaoler,
    saying nothing of the adventure.*

*A brief interlude on the return journey ~
  a quiet drowse under softly falling snowy petals
    creates a shared trust and a cherished memory.*

*My knight in shining armour drives a battered Ford
pickup, and carries the pendant that is
  my favour in the ashtray.*

Passion and Rage

19 January

"It's going to be difficult."
You said it first, and were
* not only right*
*   but prophetic.*

"Stolen moments" is such
* a cliché and not always*
*   accurate ~ say instead*
"manufactured time"
*   like the alibis around it*
* ~ "manufactured truths"*

Which version of reality do
* you want, do I want:*
And which are we keeping?

{Lying in bed before you sleep, which
* version of your day replays in your mind?}*

16 February
You breeze by
  throw out a line and walk on

Everything stops
  frozen in white heat

My heart floods my brain and stops beating
My brain, racing as you drew near, refuses any
  input not from you and gives output in
    grudging monosyllables.

Our quick and easy repartee' has died ~
(I care too much now about what I say and
  how you reply to speak so lightly as once we did.)

~ It's been almost five minutes since you've gone
My pulse is nearly down to normal and I suppose
  my thought processes will soon clear

How long before this madness no longer shakes me
  each time we meet?

17 February

We never did talk much ~
  mostly we didn't have to talk ~
    we just "knew"

But now that I don't see you alone
  I find myself "looking for meaning"   *in*
everything you do
    (or don't) say ~

Witness, for example, my sad
  comment on retrieving my heart ~
"Let's get this over with"
I was certain you wanted a break.

Suddenly, this broken pendant has
  come to be a stand-in for broken hearts
I'd tried to guess your thoughts and failed
  ~not for the first time lately
Actually, I liked not wearing my heart ~
  you were in care and control of it
    and I fancied it a symbolic tie between us
      even in the absence of our old understanding.
But I let it go and untied it,
    and you let me,
      and that's a shame.

18 February

I've been so selfish
  (now I see it ~ too late on all counts)
It's not so much that I really
  wanted the "best of both worlds" as that
I've been frozen between them.
Is "trying again to work things out"
  an example of true Courage or Cowardice?
This age in which I find myself, this world
  seems to call me courageous for taking no action,
    which seems only cowardly for me ~
      taking the easier road as usual ~
  against my heart, against my intuition,
    yet in step with this farcical society.
What's to be proud of in that?
The time is coming to ACT, to Break Away.
Don't wait for a "right time" ~ Make it Right.
All along, I've known there can be no "leaving for"
  anyone but for me ~ I know that now more than ever.
And I'll admit that you were happy before knowing me
and
  deserve so much more than I can give you just now.
So go, and know I bid you happiness, health, and peace.
Know, too, that although others will care for you
  "better" and seem to love as much, no one
    could ever care more for you than I do today.

22 February

Confusion reigns still.
Nearly a month has passed
* So why am I amazed to hear*
*   your suggestion that I*
* should "change my attitude"?*
Much of my surprise
* arises from hearing you actually*
*   speak anything so clearly to me.*
Until now, I've had the luxury of
* pretending I've been misreading your*
*   oh-so-subtle intimations*
*   that our intimate days are over.*
No longer.
Just as I finally have the time
* and energy to give you within my grasp,*
I've lost all hold on you (small as it ever was).
All the questions I have
* now are inconsequential ~*
Whatever the true answers,
* you seem to have predetermined*
*   the outcome: nothing more.*
If I can only keep quiet a while longer,
* maybe I'll get beyond this often*
*   overwhelming need to touch you at least once more,*
*   and then no longer.*

Passion and Rage

24 March

There are days, seemingly random,
  but no less intense for the inconstancy,
    when I must run ~ for a time.

The distance between us has become
  hard and cold as a terrible expanse of steel
~ with distorted reflections
  alternately laughing and scowling back at us
~ perfectly polished edges so sharp
  I nearly cry out in pain from the invisible cuts
    each time I try to find you and
      grasp instead only steely blades.

So I turn away again ~ and run sometimes
  to put a sort of insulation around this
    cruel distance that is all we share anymore.

Yet there are days
  when I miss you enough to risk the pain
    on the off-chance I could engender enough warmth to
      melt this steel wall into those links
we'd just begun to forge ~
  together instead of apart ~
    apart and lonely.

25 March

YOU MAKE YOUR CHOICES...

    ...

       ...

         ... AND THEN YOU LIVE WITH
  THEM.

  AND EVERY DAY

YOU CONTINUE THIS PLAY

  YOU MAKE YOUR CHOICE

    ALL OVER AGAIN!

14 April

There's still so much in my pen that I want to write to you but
  what good does it do anymore?
Not only will you almost
  certainly never read anything I've written
    so far, but now you
      seem so far away from even caring at all.
So why do I waste my ink on this lost cause?
Because, quite honestly and obviously, I still care
~ for you and about you. And each time I
  think of telling you so, I'm afraid to
    hear that awful phrase ("Can we still be friends?"),
      to which my heart
  cries out the so inevitable
    answer ("Certainly not!").
Rather than be forced to face each day
  without hope for us, I remain silent.
The curse is that these impulses are building and
  I'm afraid I'll explode
    someday very soon, clearly and without
      equivocation say how I feel,
  leaving what little balance that now
    exists between us
      absolutely shattered.

<u>30 April</u>

"I'm over him," I tell myself ~
No more writing
No more dreams
No more silent tears
And I almost believe it.
Then I face an overload ~
We sit side-by-side at luncheon
~ too close and I can smell the warmth of your skin
(How can I help remembering caresses once given?)
You ask me to help you
~ it's Friday evening & there's no one I'd rather be near
My hopes for intimate conversation fade as you focus,
  not on me, but on the task at hand
    from start to finish.

I'm alone in the dark again
  with my thoughts refusing to calm enough for sleep
    dancing daydreams in the night ~ all of you, of us
By three-thirty, exhaustion takes over
  and finally I sleep

But you are there in the nightdreams as well.

26 May

The next phase is now upon me.
I've moved up from catatonia around you
  to become an absolute pest
~ and not only around you, but
  around our friends ~ about you.
I know (it's quite obvious) that my
  overt interest can
  only raise the question in their minds
Of course I realize how disastrous this could be
  for both of us.
The Story will remain safe within the controlled
  environment where we are confined.
You can't help but know by now that
  all I regret is our ending
And you've made your response Very clear
~ for now

What about tomorrow, though?
Is nothing left for us to explore?
I fear your rejection but not enough to
keep from asking.
Now I should just leave,
  leave you unalone, but incomplete ~
    for I have a part of you in my soul
    and I couldn't shake it if I tried.

Maggie Vincente

31 May

How can I possibly "get over you"
  while I continue to see you daily
And when you're not here,
  your presence lingers on and on.

I don't make it any easier for myself
  by hanging pictures of our favourite places,
    but seeing them is somehow comforting ~
I didn't make it all up

It was real ~ Very Real.
And I remember how it felt when you did
  care for me

I miss feeling you that close to my soul.

Passion and Rage

Maggie Vincente

1 June

We've both loved and left before
so I'll not shower you with childish promises
of undying devotion and faithfulness
I realize the day will come (soon, I hope)
when you fade to become only an "extra" in my
dreams instead of starring every night
when I no longer feel cold and hollow
each time I hear your name
when I cease to notice little traits in others
that bring you so quickly to my mind's eye
when I can pass the forest and not cry at the beauty
we shared there once and never will share again
when all the detailed memories begin to blur

Just as surely as I know these things,
you must surely understand and know
the day will never come
when I think of you without smiling at the sweetness
when I forget your eyes, your smile, your voice
when I regret any of our brief time together
when I cease to love you with a passion
uniquely for you all alone.

22

15 June

This is all silly ~
I've felt like writing for days,
  but the feeling is too nebulous to capture in words.
So I write this to try and spark completion.
But the feeling is still there ~ unsatisfied by my efforts.

What happened is this:
I heard from you today
  only a short message
    delivered over a great distance
And discovered that you still can make me smile!
~ No kidding!~ No surprise? ~ No decrease
  and no solution in sight ~
But knowing you thought of me
  even just a little
    has really made my week light up.

04 July

Why am I
  even the least bit surprised
    that your faucets are backward
Hot means cold and warm is
  just a sweet illusion
Is the thrill of chase
  the ecstasy of capture
    or the sweet taste of the kill
  enough to justify the game
    and the morning after breath
Who is this woman
What hold does she purport to
  exert on your person
Does she even know I exist
  except in her most knowing feminine intuition,
    sensing that "her" man is not truly hers
I am so very tempted
  to wish her luck of you
    and bid her Godspeed
  in her quest to own a piece of you

18 July

I thought you would always be in my heart,
  but I was wrong
You're in my mind
You're in my soul
But where I thought I'd find you still in my heart
  I've found only a jagged hole
        (How poetic…)
I miss lots of things about you these days
  and one of the painful gaps is the loss
    of your special friendship
As you may have noticed,
  lately I'm having trouble
  inviting such from you
I've been mourning your absence in my love life
  and carefully ignoring the potential for a new phase
~ "just friends"

to be (continued) or not to be (continued)…
  what is the answer?

Maggie Vincente

21 July

You should(?) be flattered ~
You've made such an indelible impression
that I still write (and dream) of you all these
many months later. Yet I understand you are
not pleased by this tribute.
In fact, my guess (since you refuse to
say anything not absolutely necessary)
is that it annoys you greatly.
Perhaps I've finally reached the wall
~ if I stop here, I accept our parting and
  our lives go on in opposite directions
~ if I scale the wall, I could easily fall into the pit
  on the other side, known as the Abyss of Obsession.
At the moment, it seems safe only to stand, quite still
  and still hopeful of being drawn back, facing the wall,
neither crossing over nor moving beyond you.
I'm weary of this limbo-land~
who would have known letting go would be so hard?
All the right conditions have been created
~ we never spend time alone together anymore
~ our sparkling conversations are now flat and tense
~ both of us are (happily?) otherwise occupied.
But the sun still turns on when you enter the room
  and time stops each time your eyes flash a rare smile
    and I know better, but I'm still in love with you.

Passion and Rage

Maggie Vincente

6 September
At first I thought, "We need to talk."
As the day wore on, it became apparent that
* you need to talk and I need to listen*
What's going on here?!?
I've spent all these months in hard training
~ training myself not to feel this way anymore
~ training even to keep you from my dreams
I was finally beginning to handle it
~ not very well yet, but learning
And now, my carefully constructed
* façade of indifference is crumbling with*
*   each ever-stronger beat of this traitorous heart*
What's going on with you?
I was nearly resigned to your coldness to me
Then, seemingly out of the blue,
* you turn so warm that I melt under your gaze*
I know,
* you would have explained on the ride back*
*   if only I'd let you take me home*

7 September

Don't do this to me
I'm just getting over you
  learning to be without you in my days or nights
I'm not strong enough to resist you
  or even to decide not to resist you
First you pay me a clear-spoken compliment
  with time even given me to accept
Next you initiate a soft-spoken discussion
  (no tense voices, no harsh words)
Then you pay an extended visit to my new quarters
  silently appraising the décor
    (but I'm too bewildered to speak)
Moreover, all of these events take place in
  very close physical proximity to me
  (it's been a long time~ forgive me if I blush)
Finally, you present a thoughtful offer of your escort
  on the return leg of our journey
    before I could have need to ask anyone else
Thank you, but no, and please ask again
  someday when I've found my voice and courage.

8 September

Enlightening...
How refreshing to ask honest questions,
  even hypothetically, and
    actually receive straight answers from you
It's so incredibly easy to be with you ~
  why does it have to be so difficult?
But then, I'm the one who insists on
  making this complicated, right?
~ by offering what I can't truly give
(and you don't want yet anyway)
~ by asking for more than you can give
(and I couldn't take yet anyway)

The question I keep coming back to is this ~
  why should I accept all of the risks
    for only part of the rewards?
That would be illogical for me, right? ~
  which is why you keep saying not to think so much
And if logic was the only factor in this decision,
  the answer would be "Thanks for the Memories"

But my emotions do insist on being heard
~ where you're concerned, they want control of me
I want to be with you, but can I settle for even
  less than what we had last year?

9 September

I already have wonderful,
  vivid memories of being with you
    and maybe I should be content with those
    and not risk trying again.
You see, I've grown to love other things about you
  over the past year, even as I worked on
  "falling out of love with you"
(a different animal altogether).
On days we didn't speak except to argue,
  I'd hear your laugh in the next room (that laugh!),
    instantly melting my anger.
On days you were in an obviously good mood
  and happened to smile at me or throw a
    lighthearted comment my way, I'd smile
    for a while remembering what a good
friend you can be.
On days we all spent together,
  tossing around illogical ideas for adventures,
suddenly you'd say something calmly and
sure of yourself, and no argument could be raised
    against your usually brilliant point.
I feel better when you are happy ~
  whether because of someone else
is almost irrelevant.
There is a balance and a clarity here.

10 September

"I don't need in-depth relationships right now."
Thought I'd better
  write this down so I won't
    let myself forget that you
      actually used those words to me.
No matter what complications are resolved,
  no matter what I may wish,
    those are certain words which leave
      no room for misunderstanding or compromise.
I had pushed this so far into the back of
  my mind because of what I wished to be true
Perhaps that is why I've felt so uncomfortable
  trying to get back in touch with you~
    you've closed your heart to me~
I can't get in.
I was willing, I thought,
  to play the game lightheartedly,
    but I can't play if I'm not allowed to love you.
We've tried this before and both lost
  (and I nearly lost my mind afterward)
How could I think of playing
  with even less to win?

11 September

Another fantasy
  takes shape and shadow
My eyes close and for a moment
  you're sitting across from me
    leaning against this sturdy pine
your blue eyes smiling in the
  sunlight filtering through the branches
this brown needle carpet is soft
  as I lie back, watching you watching me
this spot, this oasis betwixt and between
  so many crowded campsites, is so peaceful
time here moves as slowly as we like
  and we have so much of it ~ all to ourselves
The earth moves on a bit and a
  sunbeam breaks through and lands between us
We move closer to it and to each other
  the warmth is hypnotic and
    together we sleep
  my head on your belly, yours rests on my thigh
Heaven is real and now and here~
  none dare disturb us but rabbits and raccoons.

Maggie Vincente

12 September

Thanks for waiting~
Sometime in the last few days I must
  have reached a decision
(My mind is calmer now and open to sounds
  and sights surrounding me in this forest.)
Memories have come clearly
  to me in dreams
    of what I've said and done
      and not done, but wanted so to do.
The negative motivation is less now
  than a year ago, but the positive incentive
    seems to be greater.
There is less hope for more from you,
  but more understanding of what there is.
Just two weeks ago, I was
  fantasizing about the chance
    you offered just two days ago.
I decided months ago to be with you
  if I had a real chance again~
    it just took me a few days to remember that
      and turn that promise to myself
  into a promise to you.

23 September

Yesterday I almost threw it all away.
How would you react, I wonder,
  if faced with such unwavering evidence
    of my feelings for you as show up in
      this precious packet of words?

Fortunately, I returned to my senses and
  remembered that, since no good would
    probably come from putting such
knowledge into your hands,
  why again should I tell you
    what you don't want to hear?!
Answer: I won't (for now).

Maybe I'll just leave it with you
  as I go away from this place
Then if you want to get rid of this journal,
  fine~ just please burn it rather than
    tossing it aside for others to read and be hurt.

07 October

Last night
I looked up as I brushed
my teeth, and saw in the mirror
a look in my eyes that
scared and saddened me.
My masque of contentment
had slipped away~
no one else could see~
the look was that seen in
the eyes of zoo animals~
lost, confused, caged but too
dispirited to fight it anymore.
As I looked at that look
(feeling an objective observer
somehow),
all I could think was that
this one will soon die if not freed.
Such a strange thought, and yet
so obvious and full of pathos~
there was no room for other interpretation.

It was like I had caught myself unaware.

<u>08 October</u>

God, I feel so high on life now!
It's almost dark, dusk actually,
  and yet all I see is light.
It's as though I've been reborn!
"I'm back!" I scream to the skies~
It feels so very good finally to have made a
  decision and to actually have done
    something about it.
It must have been right.
I know I can handle anything that
  fate throws my way from now on and on.
My eyes, my whole self, must show
  how wondrously aware and awake
    my mind is after seeing you today.
I've broken free and am burdened no longer
  ~no more darkness grips my heart or
    shadows my eyes ('twas there just yesterday).
My spirit, my will, is mine and strong,
  vital and viable and will not die after all.
I haven't felt this high on life in years!

09 October

So this is what daily life looks like
  through happy eyes~
Colours are deeper and patterns sharper,
  more visible~ light seems to reflect off
    everything in sight!

I wonder if I look different to anyone else?
How can this gladness not show in my face,
  my eyes, my movements, at least in my voice?

I suppose this could be the
  excitement of again spending a few
    precious seconds alone with someone
I care for deeply and missed more than I knew.

You make me happy so often~
  I wish I could return the favour.

<u>10 October</u>

As exactly as I can see the dramatic difference
     between being in love, and loving someone...

"In love" connotes a Love Is Blind attitude
 (and don't tell me what I don't want to hear).
"Loving" connotes Acceptance of everything
 known and true interest in further discovery.

"In love" thinks perfection has been found.
"Loving" knows better and loves still more.

"In love" encompasses the negatives
 attributed too often to Love~ capriciousness,
selfishness, obsessiveness, jealousy, ad nauseum

"Loving" encompasses the positives, known and
yet to know~ honesty, devotion, caring without
 reservation, trust, commitment, ad infinitum...

So, in answer to your question,
 I'm not "in love" with anyone.
Aren't you glad I love you instead?

Passion and Rage

Maggie Vincente

31 October

If I leave without you tomorrow,
  if I manage to fly away free,
    would you ever remember me?
Sometimes I think you will.
This morning, amidst all the teasing and
  comments on my costume,
    one voice was noticeably absent.
Now I'm glad you saved your opinion
  for my ear alone (so sweetly said!)~
    and then you were gone (bittersweet now).
Don't laugh, but this reminds me of that day
  last fall when you came in and I greeted you
    with a whispered "Welcome Home" and a
      quick kiss on your cheek~
The look on your face then, in your eyes,
  is just how I feel now.
Once again, you save the day!

04 November

The dreams are back with sweet vengeance...
  all the fantasies to match yours and more
    and I can't wait to sleep each night
      where I can make time stand still
  or move oh-so-slowly as you taught me.
When I awaken, I always wonder~
  "why only in dreams?"
I honestly believe, after all this time and trial,
  that given the chance, we could be great.
But we won't be "given" the chance,
  and there's always risk, isn't there, in trying
    to cross complicating barriers?
Maybe without anger as an impetus,
  I don't have the courage to take that risk~
It's time I admit to a desperate fear of
  being alone and unloved and unneeded.
Will I continue to let fear rule my life or
  begin anew, letting dreams guide me to where
    sleep is for rest, not for escape?
My friends remember a different me & wonder
  what happened~
I know.

07 November

Waiting.

Whole lifetimes spent waiting.

Waiting for the right quest.

Waiting for the right person.

Waiting for the right move.

Waiting for the right moment
  to begin to live for now
    and wait no more.

It's so much easier to wait
  than to risk life in the present.

07 November…still

So many dreams.
Even the repeats are incredible.
When do they begin to come true?

He's so sure of me.
Would he even be hurt if he knew what I don't feel?

You're so unsure of me. If you knew what I feel,
* what would you say? what would you do?*
*   what would you feel? anything?*

You play it so close~ would you ever let me in?

14 November

A beautiful sunset,
  infinitely brighter and more colourful than
    that portrayed on the painting in this room,
  lights up the lakeview from my window, and
    for a moment, I'm back in my childhood home
  watching this brilliance on the river~
How I wish I could share either sunset with you
  ~ and future sunrises as well.

See?   My dreams and desires are finally
  becoming more focused, even if all my
    decisions aren't so clear yet.

There are so many incredible sights, sounds,
  emotions, thoughts, experiences I'd like for us
    to share ~ somehow it's not just a wish anymore
~ more positive, more possible now, somehow.

Sometimes I even dare to believe that
  we'll actually get there together.
What do you think?
One year ago today~~~

Passion and Rage

15 November

Once again I've spent too much time
  on the fantasy and not enough in reality
And so the dream as well as the day
  lays in pieces at my feet~
    like my pendant that broke again (an omen?)
Simultaneously another mini-escape plan
  (from you?) has failed
So I'm stuck with no easy excuses to instantly
  solve all my problems
Perhaps I really will have to make my own
  decisions and take action on them alone.
I know you can't help (and should not) and I
  won't ask it of you~
But it doesn't seem the same thing to ask for
  your support of me in my decision.
Can't I ask that of you as my friend?

<u>16 November</u>

It still astounds me that you seem so unaware
  of how very much I love you.
Maybe you really don't care, or think you
  know better than to care.
Either possibility is unacceptable (like I have
  the right to decide for you what is and is not).
Either way, I know I could change your mind
  by changing my circumstance, but this is
    too important for creative manipulations~
If you care or when you care is for you to know.
And..., and if and when you do,

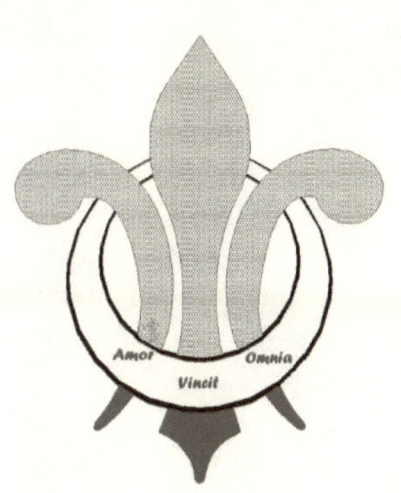

I'm taking no chances.
I won't mess it up.
I'll be me and you'll be you ~
I'll do everything I can
to never let you down.
I'll support your endeavours.
I will believe in you as you.
I will defy attacks
on our magic.
I will share with you
laughter, dreams, adventures,
"learning experiences",
friends, family
peace, all, my love.

it will..., no, WE will never end.

14 December

In a flurry at the first
  Down to a trickle as the evening wears ~
My dance card approaches filled
  without your name
As it grows clear
  that the absence of you
may give rise to comment
more than your presence,
  you take my hand
  and the magic of this dance is born
   amid the candleglow
Swirling ever faster
then slowly as we draw more near
who could fault us for succumbing
  to the magic of our dance

03 Year, 06 January

To Myself:
Show us all the new you
~be happy for you, for him, for them.

Admit that you're human
   ~that sometimes you have to give up
   and try something new,
like enthusiasm with "now" and
   peace with yourself for all that you've been
blessed to have known (look at how much
   wiser you've grown in the past two years).

The time for depression is past
~say goodbye to the tears and fears and wants
~greet gladly the smiles, laughter and joy of
   each moment.

You knew the answer a year ago, when you
   were told to "change your attitude".   How true
and how stubborn and spoiled of you to wait
   so long to accept such wise advice.

Maggie Vincente

<u>Quarter Turn</u>

"Here's a quarter," as she flipped a coin onto his lap.

"What's this for?" he said to her back.

She was leaving.

"I don't know," came the cryptic yet routine reply.

All week she elaborated on
the 'could have-would have-should have' theme
with snappy replies and soulful witticisms...

Of course, by that time, the chance to say something
  memorable or even meaningful was long gone,
and any attempt to reopen the discussion
would be met rightfully with ridicule.

Originally, she had intended to say,
  AS the coin tumbled through the air,
"just in case you want to make a call tonight."

But she thought better of it only
  AFTER the money had left her fingertips.

Passion and Rage

*The next thought was a modified
"just in case you need to make that call someday."*

*So IT came out,
  that stand-by, fill-in line she used
when too shy or too cute or not ready to say
  what she really felt.*

*But the problem was that she DID know and it
  changed nothing, even after all this time and trial.*

*So here's a quarter that I'm sure I
would have used to call you sooner or later...*

8 January

Maggie Vincente

<u>29 January</u>

Limited time offer only (these ½ weekends)
When you're ready to deal with it, call me (truly!)
Why do you push me to ask, only to refuse again
You're pretty brave to ask, when it sounds
  like I'm making plans.
I'm pretty naive to have actually waited for you again
I agree my life now is bizarre, but reading you is tough
You asked about my fantasies; you don't want to know.
I wish a hundred years had passed; would it be easier?
    I love you and that's all I know.
When I said I had to leave, you knew I couldn't handle it.
I could be really good at the work if I could concentrate.
I used to be proud of who I am; this inferiority trash <u>is</u>!
I hate guessing your mind; how do I get past your wall?
This tiredness is overwhelming, so I pack another box
Reconcile: Don't run from problems & Just start fresh.
Why do we stay silent when we have a chance to talk
(after you walked in and left barely ½ an hour later)?
I want so badly sometimes to say, "just never mind",
but it wouldn't matter if I did ~ I'd still care and would
have driven in another wedge.
            Please help me out of the trap.

Passion and Rage

17 February

The dream is over now,
  it's only lingering effects
    attraction, not affection.
I think we've used each other
  long enough.
Yes, we've had fun (we're good, eh?).
Time to move into real life
  and true feelings.
So you two go on with your
  promising, exciting life -
and we two might try to go
  back to where we used to be.
If you're right and it's my choice,
  I'm ready to grow up a little,
    how about you?   Are you game?
It's your choice, too.
But I do know that if you had
  truly wanted to understand,
    you would have read all of this by now.
The fact that you have not tells me you're holding
  this pawn in a poor power play.
Well, I'm taking control of my own life now
  ~ the power is in my hands again.

20 February

You and I are long overdue for a good argument.
Problem is - you don't care enough to argue
with me (or are you scared?)
Do you have any idea
* what happens when your name comes up*
*   and you're not around, but I am?*
I promote you, I compliment you,
* and more, I defend you, still, always ~*
*   for all the time since I got here (and I've had*
many occasions to do so, believe me!).
Yet you, somewhere along the way,
* forgot how to do the same for me.*
Worse yet, now I find you're insulting me?!
How long has this been your practice?
All the while, you're sweetness and light and fun
* when you're with me ~ I thought I was the actor.*
That's worse than disrespectful ~ that's just plain
* nasty and I can't believe it's coming from you.*
If I've done or said things to anger or hurt you,
* why won't you bring them to me?*
What is your fear, that keeps your apparent sudden
* hatred of me hidden from my view*
("a big scene"? ~come on...)
The worst part of this is that the dreamer in me
keeps hoping you can truthfully deny all this.
The realist in me doubts it, though.

Maggie Vincente

21 February

What goes through your head when you come back
to me (or is just pleasure-centers doing the thinking)?
Nearly all your friends say you love her,
  but that's not love as I've ever heard it.
You can't truly expect (can you?),
  after knowing me all this time,
  that I'll actually accept the tidbits you throw my way,
like those empty-headed girl-children you gather near,
  grateful for something so shallow and vacuous.
Yes, you did change the rules, not recently, though.
Last fall when all between us started up again, the
  tenor had changed, only I was too full of hope to see.
Whatever true feeling we shared at first has been
  markedly and unceasingly withheld in Act II of this
play in which we've found ourselves engaged.
That frightening grin when you asked "can you take it?"
  looked hopeful that I can't (are you trying to drive me
insane?). What did I do to make you hate me so?
Love you so?   The man I first learned to love,
  the man I thought you were, would not take advantage
so cruelly of a love given so freely.
No promises were ever exchanged.
We cared too much to lie. It's obvious that my only
choice is to cut these now tawdry ties between us.
It's the hardest thing I've ever been assigned,
  but I'm trying; Lord, I'm trying so hard.

08 March

You could have had it all.
I was willing to give you my everything,
  the world, the moon, the seas.
All you had to do was accept it all.
You chose instead to hate and to hurt. Why?
Because I loved you, you hated me?
You have no idea the good life you missed.
No one has ever had all my best - no one.
You could have had it all.
A long time ago, you told me to be content,
  that I was getting the best of you.
I didn't believe it then and I don't believe it now.
You certainly got my worst moods and
boundless uncertainties.
Others say you took advantage of my feelings.
That implies a lack of my consent, which isn't so.
I was willing to give anything you asked, always
  hoping you'd ask for more, just to be with you,
to be close in the only way you'd opened for me.
You've been trying only to destroy my love for so
  long now that you may have finally found the key.
What you seem to have forgotten, because I know
  you understood in the beginning of us, is that my
trust is infinitely more rare and more precious a gift
than my love. There are many in this life whom I love.
But there are very few I trust like I <u>instantly</u> trusted you.

09 March

Don't you remember when I said
  "I've never been wrong"?
I wasn't speaking of love ~
  I've been wrong plenty of times in love,
    and if this is one of those times,
  so be it.
I was referring to my rare, complete trust in you.
I've never been wrong in trusting someone before
  and it's quite a blow to comprehend
being wrong about you.
I still don't believe it
even as I felt like screaming when last we spoke,
I want to beg you, please, to deny it,
to tell me I'm wrong, to give me some other reason.
                    But it won't happen.
I guess I have no choice
  but to accept it.
That's got to be the hardest pain
  in this world.
It goes so much deeper in the soul
  than death of a love.

Maggie Vincente

<u>20 March</u>

"...if I'm up to it"!?!
I've been waiting for a good
  opportunity to argue with you
    for MONTHS now.
How clever of you to try to stage
  the showdown at a totally inappropriate time!
Besides, why on earth do I have to be
  "up to it" to argue with you?
Do you plan to launch so
  severe a personal attack that
    you fear I may not survive it?
You've been attacking me in secret
  for many months now ~
    I've survived that, haven't I?
If you want this battle,
  you'd better make the time quickly.
Because I'm almost too
  exhausted to try anymore to reach you.
Yes, you've almost beaten me -
  I almost don't care anymore.
You've done a splendid job at
  killing my love for you.
Now you've nearly killed something
  infinitely more important and
    definitely much stronger ~
    my faith in you.

29 March

Love means knowing when you have
  to say you're sorry.
Now that you seem a bit less full of rage,
  do you have room to accept an apology from me?
I won't pretend I've figured it out,
  because you remain the only soul who knows
    what it is that has hurt you so.
But I will admit that I've been
  far less than fair with you.
And there have been many things between us
  that could easily have been misinterpreted ~
    how could there not be,
      when we're so careful not
  to say too much,
  to feel too much,
  to show too much,
    and lose the hand.
Well, I broke the rules,
  and you changed the rules ~
    rules have never worked well for us, have they?
Whether we have the chance to make new rules
  together or not, I apologize for
    all I've said and done, or not, that hurt you.
I never wanted to, never meant to, and I'm sorry.

30 March

Hurrah!
You're actually speaking to me again,
  even when you don't need to say something!
At this point,
  even going back to (forward to?)
    having you not give a damn about me
      is a major improvement over you hating me...
        That's been really tough to take.

'Don't know if this means
  "brighter days lay ahead",
but today was brighter than yesterday,
  and yesterday brighter than the day before that.
'Too early to declare a trend,
  but I will say I'm smiling a lot more this week.

07 April

I think I'm up to
  repeating myself in writing
But it's been so long
  since our last "personal" fight
    (or so acknowledged)
  that I've not had the chance
    to speculate to you personally
    (only on paper).

You've got to stop this revenge business ~
  Not because it's hurting me
    (which I know is the point, after all)
  Now it's threatening to backfire
    and hurt you even more.
{I know vengeful schemes have a way of doing that
in fables, but this time it's true in real life as well.}
Your colleagues and others have
  begun to notice and question your seemingly
    unfounded "misbehavior" toward me and think,
      at best, that it's highly irresponsible of you.

Don't let yourself get caught in this now,
  especially if you're trying to
  teach some secret lesson to me.

13 April

You did it again.
This afternoon, I answered the phone
  and heard the sound of you.
I'd swear the room got brighter at the
  instant you spoke my name.
But it was probably just the light
  reflecting off the tears that
    fill my eyes when I hear
  the angry distance in your tone lately
    (directed only to me).
How melodramatic!
The cold facts are these:
  I can't be with you if I stay here;
        I won't be with you if I leave;
You appear to wish I'd left long ago; and
I don't want to be here except to be near you.
None of these leaves room for us
  to be together,
    so why do I remain?
Why throw away this secure,
  apparently happy life
    for the chance to be alone forever?
As far as anyone else can tell,
  my life is perfectly fine.

23 April

Patience, child...
Don't be in such a rush for resolution.
Just because you've got it all figured
  doesn't mean he can take it all at once.
The whole idea is still new to him.
Give it time to sink in before
  you bring it up again.
Learn from all the mistakes made earlier.
If you push too hard,
  the villain's grip will only tighten
    (or snap, sending pieces of you
  flying violently in all directions).
You should know by now
  how to handle this delicate negotiation
    and "win".
This mediation is too crucial
  for haste and mistakes
    to lose it for you.
Determination can deliver
  the results you desire
    if you'll only have enough...
Patience.

Passion and Rage

<u>26 April</u>

"I still remember everything you said
  (e.g., "It won't be easy").
You were absolutely right,
  although it may have been a
   self-fulfilling prophecy of sorts.
And yet I'm glad we met
  and knew one another.
I would not change the events
  that brought me here
   into your play, for not
  meeting you would always have been
   a disquieting hole in my life.
Maybe there is truth in the
  "better to have loved & lost, than not" adage.
I will remember the good things we knew
  long after the pain has faded (it will fade, right?).
I'm glad I wanted and needed you,
  and certainly I'm glad I loved you
   (the highs were well worth all the lows).
I will remember, too, and be glad for the moment,
  just a brief, glorious moment,
   so very long ago now,
  when you wanted and needed me
   and even loved me ~ just for a moment.
"How could I ever forget?"

18 May

26 April seems so long ago.
Although I've not written since,
  you have been constantly in my thoughts,
    and of course, in all my dreams.
Wish You Were Here...
Things all look brighter
  in this sunny place ~
Somehow here all my dreams actually
  seem like real possibilities.
Maybe I've just been able to smooth
  all the rough edges between us ~
    but only in my mind,
    and nothing will have changed when I get back.
When I do get back,
  I'll return your prized picture
    to its customary spot,
  retrieving my place marker-in-code.
Wondered if you'd be furious with me
  for taking it along,
    but decided that was unlikely
    (too much emotion for you toward me anymore).
So I risked the improbable wrath in
  exchange for enjoying something so sweet ~
I feel not so terminally "away" from you
  when I hold your picture.

Maggie Vincente

20 May

I miss you!
Trouble is, I miss you these days
* even when we're in the same room ~ so being*
miles away should not feel so very different.
However,
* from here I must rely on my memory*
*   to hear your laughter,*
*   see your smile,*
*   and feel the gaze of your ocean eyes.*
It's becoming increasingly obvious
* that leaving you behind,*
*   knowing it's near-definitely for Forever,*
* will be the hardest and loneliest*
*   thing I've yet to face.*
For so long now (months!),
* I've wanted to just say to you,*
*   "Come with me."*
But even if I had the nerve to ask,
* I'm sure I'd have to walk away with*
*   the sound of stone silence or*
* maybe even incredulous laughter*
*   ringing in my ears.*
I guess it really is too late for us.
{So why am I counting the days
* until I'm near you again?...}*

25 May

Never have I been
  so hard hit with a
    Profound Revelation.
Since almost "day two",
  I've laid out the pattern
    to treat you as I've been treated.
There was never such conscious intent,
  but the results are the same ~
now it's all too clear ~
  but too late for change and
    far beyond the point of salvage
(what's left to hold on to anymore?).
At least now I think I understand your anger
  with all the mindgames I threw your way.
At least now I can begin to stop
  trying to set the mood
    the chance for a reunion of souls
                ~ a reintroduction of minds
                ~ a retying of old bonds.
At least now I can accept the blame
  and accept that there can be
no forgiveness from you.

Maggie Vincente

28 May

Sunset glistens through cracks in this barn ~
Here we stood as I told you,
* finally said it aloud ~   I Love You.*
You denied it for me, said I'd get over you.
No, I'm sorry, this is not the kind of thing
one "gets over" ~
* more something one accepts and goes on.*
Loving you gives me the highest highs
* and my lowest of heartbreaking lows.*
Highs because I'm filled with joy
* just knowing you breathe.*
Lows because I know soon I'll leave,
* never to see you again.*
And part of my concentration will always
be on reserve ~
* listening for news of how you are, where you are,*
*   if those might be, hope against all hope,*
*   your footsteps, your laughter outside the door ~*
feeling nothing more intensely
* than the absence from my life*
*   of the one I truly love who never*
* could love me in return.*

Passion and Rage

Maggie Vincente

30 May ~ To His Best Friend

Like most "perfect fit" phrases,
  they all come to me in a rush
    as the time to speak aloud is over ~

How can you possibly think
  I would ever do this again?
I don't think any of us could survive this again!
I can never forget;
  no one won,
    everyone was hurt,
  and all I have to show is silent wisdom

~ Perhaps most important,
  and too fragile to say aloud ~
Maybe you think you don't owe me any favours,
  but please do this for me when I'm gone...
If it ever comes up
  (and we all know it will),
Please,
  tell him the truth.

No, I will never forget what I've done here.
Neither will I forget what you've done.
Shall I tell him for you?
      Whom shall I tell instead?

06 June

I want so badly
  to get this feeling captured into words
  so that I can remind myself
    what not to do again.
For at least two weeks now,
  I've been waiting for a chance,
    even a chance of a chance,
  to apologize to you alone.
Until today, someone was always near
  or you were obviously not in the mood
    for conciliatory words from me.
Then, this afternoon, apparent opportunity
  shined on me... and I choked!
I had stepped outside, only to see you
  standing quite still (in deep thought or waiting?)
I stopped, you looked up,
  and before I could meet your eyes,
    I looked down and walked away.
I still cannot believe I said nothing!
If only I had stopped to think for a moment,
  I would likely have asked if you were all right,
    and then maybe you'd have
  listened to my apology.
The longer I stay here,
  the more idiotic and tragic this becomes.

Maggie Vincente

13 June

Please define "I don't want to play anymore"
~ If we can't do this for real, I can't do this at all
* (You were right ~ I can't take it.)*

I always knew, or suspected,
* that my acting had limits ~*
I finally found the breakdown point:
* you defined it all.*
No longer can I pretend I don't care.
No longer can I give just a token,
* afraid to show you how much I want to give.*
No longer can I survive in this futuristic
* fantasy life based on "what if" and "perhaps".*

I never claimed to want it all ~
* I just want to share what there is with you.*
I know you have so much more to give, too.
The question is not, right now,
* whether you and I can be more to each other,*
but whether we can get beyond where
* we are stopped.*

Without that, any hopes for a shared reality
* die with the fantasy.*

14 June

You almost sounded surprised
  today when we spoke ~
I wonder if you noticed the change
  in my voice?
Somewhere about noon, I had
  another Profound Revelation.
I've been extremely nervous around you lately,
  trying not to say or do the wrong thing.
I was truly terrified this morning,
  that you would start to shout at me,
    or end our conversation angrier than usual.
Enter the flash of insight ~
Worrying over what you'll do to me in your
  ever-increasing hatred (angry apathy?) will
change nothing now. (Your fury is based on my
past behaviour, not current.)
Instead, if I relax and just deal with one scene
  at a time, I can actually enjoy talking with
  you again, enjoy the sound of your voice, and
  enjoy actually doing something to
help you a bit,which is my favourite part.
And then, my voice patterns change ~
  the frantic stutter disappears,
replaced with the soft, but unmistakable
  sounds of "I miss you".   And I do.

<u>17 June</u>

True to legend,
  my luck was running in three's yesterday ~
my mother's rings resurfaced,
  a promising chance for me to leave appeared,
    and you finally did show up last evening
(wonder of wonders, we were nice to each other).
But where you are concerned,
  I seem never to be satisfied.
I lay awake 'til almost morning
  thinking of how I should have taken the chance as
we were leaving last night to sit you down alone for
  a moment and finally talk with you (last chance?).
However, I've been so morose over how selfish I've
  been to you, that it's become a part of my reality.
I didn't even think of anything other
  than the need to keep you safe on your way home.
I know you're a grown man and
take fine care of yourself.
But that's one of the privileges of loving someone ~
  worrying and protecting and
    reassuring and worrying more.
Don't be too hard on me for it; you'll not have
  to notice it but for a few days more,
    then I'll be the one on my way to a new home.

21 June

The Play Continues...
...and deliver us from ourselves,
  that we may not lead others into lunacy...
I wonder how all this would feel
  if my reasons were only the ones everyone knows.
I don't even know how to act it out anymore,
  because the real reasons have filled me with panic.
I hate what they all must think of my groundless
impatience.
But "time is of the essence" in ways I cannot
  begin to explain to anyone other than
you who know already.
And I'm burning to be moved (removed) from here,
  before I lose my nerve like I've always done before.
Who would ever believe this makes perfect sense?
I have to leave here to "leave",
  but I really don't want to leave here
    (leave him, but not you).
And you won't want me not to leave
  until I prove I can leave, if then,
    which I can only test by leaving.
No wonder I'm a frazzled bundle of nerves.
I don't like it, but I understand it.
Everyone has to believe how much I want to leave,
so no one will suspect how very much I want to stay.

27 June

Fearing no new chance
  to be alone with you long enough,
I had to make the opportunity.
Circumstances were less than ideal,
  but that's nothing new for us.
True to form, you surprised me ~
In all the scenarios I had
  envisioned for this situation,
    it never occurred to me that
  you would not listen to me.
("You don't owe me any apologies.")
Now I find I'm torn ~
  was that a comforting phrase,
    that on some level you do understand?
Or more likely, perhaps,
  that you've been immune to me
  for so long now that I can't reach you?
Either way,
  I've come away from yet another
    encounter with you
  shaking inside and out.

28 June

What would you think
 if I really got brave
  and asked you to come go with me?
Laugh if you like,
 but I'm serious, dear ~
  with you is where I'd like to be.

If only I did have the nerve and the chance
 to say it straight like that ~
You do have another option this Friday.
There's a small caravan leaving that morning
 for adventures unknown.
I happen to know the driver, and
 that no passengers have signed on as yet.
I'd wager there would be plenty of room
 for two cases and you.

Would you consider it?

Maggie Vincente

28 June ~ The Last Day

How can I say goodbye to you?
We've done this too many times before,
  and I kept coming back.
This time, the leaving is real
  and planned, and public knowledge,
    and I can't come back.
But I cannot bring myself to even
  bid you farewell ~
A flippant "'See you 'round",
  knowing we'll likely never meet again, would be
far too casual for something once so intense.
And hearing your voice deliver any serious
  goodbye   would be the final jagged cut
  to my tattered heart ~
All the lifeblood would surely drain
  immediately from my veins.
So, in addition to my other
  transgressions toward you,
    now please forgive me
  for leaving when you're away.
            ****

Except that I had no courage and so returned,
  to touch you just once more,
    but you refused to meet my eyes.
Sadness or relief?

Maggie Vincente

<u>Moving In Time ~ Changes In L'Attitudes</u>

Long-distance isn't necessarily so.
The old, familiar patterns
  where our phrases and thoughts
  flow like so much quicksilver,
    return quickly and effortlessly
      to ease our conversation.
A thousand miles apart,
  yet we remain aligned in spirit.
With other loves and lives,
  yet we remain for each other
    as no one else could ever be.

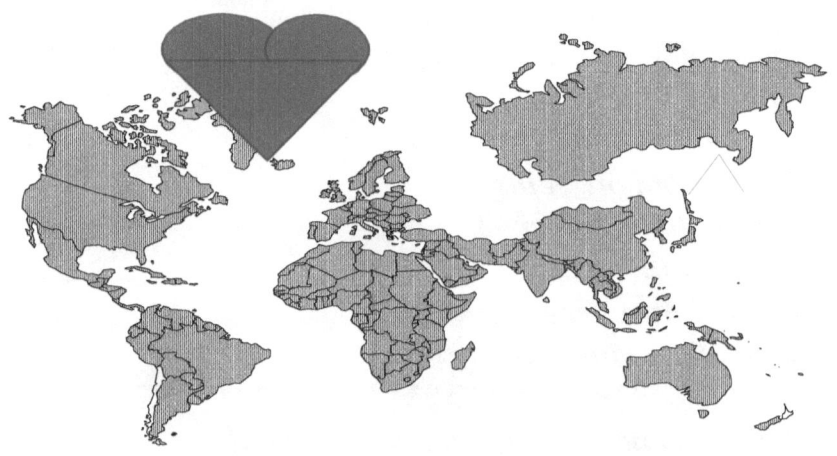

86

The Next Year ~ Colours of Memory

Your memories are vivid colours,
  while I remember them not.
Mine are so much more varied,
  like the chills that I got
    when you entered a room or
  spoke my name or picked
    me up, which you did a lot.
The sound of your laughter
  still makes me blush,
    and to touch what you've written
      can give me a rush.
I can still smell your nape
  on a cold winter's night
    when you'd been wearing your
      leather coat closed up tight.
The day that you rescued and
  and returned me, life changed.
November fourteenth lives on
  and the magic remains.
The only colour I still see
  is that of your eyes
    when your hair was light
      and you were looking at me.
For that moment, and few others since,
  we were in love and captured by bliss.

Maggie Vincente

<u>Time Tiptoes By ~ A Growing Glow</u>

Scattered calls and
  wished-for visits
    sprinkled through time
  like seeds resowing proven ground
Keeping the "us" that we knew alive
  and fed just enough to survive
Bitterness mellows with age
  and sweetness begins to seep in
    at the cracks
Hope waits poised,
  quivering liquid faith,
    glowing promises bound in distance
Which of us will be the
  first to tap into the golden possibility

Time for Us ~ Wonder of Wonders

With great anticipation, we arranged to meet
  tonight, after all these years...
It was a shock to realize that I may not have
  recognized you had we passed on the street ~
    notwithstanding that familiar charge of
  pure energy as you drew near
Your voice is unchanged (still liquid silk!),
  yet your words are vastly different
                        (wondrously so!)
Looking into your eyes over a delicious
shared repast, I saw a light not seen
before tonight ~ as though your defenses
  were being determinedly abandoned
All our seemingly accidental touches
  poured forth worlds of possibility
    which never existed before tonight ~
  as though all my old dreams were
    shared and desired now as deeply by you
The velvet petals of the rose you presented were
  rough by comparison to the softness of
your caresses and the gentle light of the moon
harsh next to the warm glow in your face
as you kissed me long and deep.
At last, the language of our loving
  expanded to capture the words so long awaited.
Wonder of wonders, "I Love You's" are exchanged.

Maggie Vincente

Time So Still ~ Passion and Rage

As two halves of one body,
  we have no choice in the joining
    of our fingers, lips, breath after breath ~
Your kisses surround me
  until the chill river winds recall
    to mind our stance in full view...
A passing carriage transports our reunion
  to more suitable quarters, where the rooms
    are lit only by our glowing hearts ~
As tender touches from remembered hands
  release hot flowing tears,
    rage at our wasted years apart
  bursts through practiced controls
    and I'm your girl all over again.
Cautious walls lay in rubble at our feet,
  felled by the death of anguish,
    and the rebirth of indestructible passion.
Eagerly we reach to entwine
  our too-long separated selves ~
    reliving an ageless ecstasy
  that is ours alone,
    life to life,
      throughout all time.
One hundred years begins and ends
  with the union of our souls tonight ~

<u>Time Shifts Forever</u>

And finally,
 finally, we have now
   completed the connection.
The missing piece
  of this so very troubling
   puzzle has been added ~
thank you for finding
   the courage to contribute
    such a beautiful gift.
Your honesty and
  genuine expression
    have given to my life
such an incredible freedom
    that has been so very missing.
Until now,
  the battle raged quietly,
    unattended beneath the surface.
Until now,
  the questions burned in the darkness,
    and the pain, though subtle, remained.
And now,
  the struggle is ended,
    the questions have answers,
      and the wounds are healed with love.

<u>Time and Again</u>

On my way to peaceful slumber at last,
* I can delight in remembering all the piquant*
details of our first-ever genuine date ~
In the space of a few short hours,
* we trudged through all the hurt*
*   and confusion of our unshared past ~*
* putting it truly to rest in newly shared empathy*
We then traveled clearly into this evening
* discovering that, while appearances have altered,*
*   how we see one another has not.*
Despite our long divergent paths,
* in this one enchanted moment,*
*   the magic has all come back to us now*
~ all the intense hunger
~ all the aching tenderness
~ all the synchronicity of
our unseverable lives

A crystalline passage emerges
* to embrace the truth of this*
undying love ~
* complete, immutable,*
*   wondrous in its simplicity.*
~ And a red, red rose
lingers at the door as
* never our goodbyes are spoken.*

<u>Finis ~ The Final Chapter</u>

We can never again be severed in spirit,
  yet irrevocable choices forbid us this union.
We have seen now the danger of
  allowing even a whisper of flame near
the tamped embers of our long-denied love.
We must run, farther and faster than ever we've run,
  away from the one thing that can destroy us ~
that can, in one instant, annul the sense of our lives.
This journal will end and be lost to history.
Besides, how could I write Chapter 2 without you?
Chapter 1 ended many years ago
  as we went our solitary ways.
The plot has diverged and our characters' lives
  developed along vastly different paths.
Yet our separated stories remain
  always a part of the same book,
    tied together as surely as any
      leather-bound volume of poetry or prose.
This lifetime is full with the
  unmistakable knowing that you loved me.
In a parallel universe, I know we remain
together and share life passionately.
Yet in this world we know,
  our lives are whole and complete
    and nothing, not even you, is missing.

Maggie Vincente

<u>Time For You ~ Fare Well, Brave Knight</u>

Too volatile to be pleasant
* and too perilous to savour long,*
*   our absolute reunion must needs end here.*

Perhaps you and I have settled old intrigues,
* lingering from lives previously shared.*

Perhaps my Prince Charming will yet appear,
* now that I am whole again.*

You, my valiant Knight,
* are an Incurable Romantic ~*
Perhaps an incurably romantic damsel, who
* appreciates that thornbushes have roses,*
*   will yet reach and rescue you ~*
Yours is an Amazing and Beautiful spirit
* and you have earned much happiness.*

Fare well, my dear, sweetest Knight.

Passion and Rage

Maggie Vincente

~ *The End* ~

Maggie Vincente

~ *Reprise* ~

"...the day will never come
when I think of you without smiling at your sweetness
when I forget your eyes, your smile, your voice
when I regret any of our brief time together
when I cease to love you with a passion
uniquely for you all alone..."

~~~

"...souls once torn apart...
reunited, for a brief time only"

~ MAGGIE VINCENTE

www.ingramcontent.com/pod-product-compliance
Lightning Source LLC
Chambersburg PA
CBHW021126130626
46554CB00002B/887